BAD BOY BILLIONAIRE DADDY

AN ENEMIES TO LOVERS SURPRISE PREGNANCY ROMANCE

EVERLEIGH GREEN

EVERLEIGH GREEN PUBLISHING LLC

HE'S MY EX-BOSS, TWICE MY AGE, MY FAKE FIANCÉ AND NOW… MY BABY DADDY.

My infuriatingly sexy boss has hired me to be his fake fiancé at his family wedding to appease his dying grandmother.

I know deep down I'll regret it, but he's desperate and I need the cash.

The man I've locked horns with is now my partner in a charade that's as thrilling as it is dangerous.

His smoldering looks are unraveling my defenses faster than his ripped forearms are unraveling my skirt.

In the heat of the night, the lines get blurred between business and pleasure.

And as his gruff exterior softens, I can't deny I'm falling for him… fast.

I'm not just his pretend fiancé, I'm the woman who might just change him.

Just when I thought things couldn't get messier, now I have to tell him that this baby in my belly… belongs to him.

"I don't know how the hell I let you talk me into this," I said into my cell phone to my best friend, Callie.

"You didn't exactly need much persuasion when you heard that one week's work would bag you a hundred thousand dollars," Callie reminded me. "And it's barely even work."

"I know, but when I agreed to it, it was just an idea. Now it's real and I actually have to go through with it," I said.

"Ok, Lena, breathe," Callie said. "Remember what I said? All the guy wants is a pretend fiancé in public so his family stay off his back and his old grandmother thinks he's found the one and can die happy. That's it. He's not the sort of person who needs to pay for sex. Honest, he's smoking hot, just your type. You're basically going to have a nice week in a nice hotel with good food and decent people. And you get paid for it."

"You're starting to sound like you regret offering me the job," I said with a soft laugh.

"Girl I would take your hand off for this one, but you

would never handle the other client. He's … messier shall we say," Callie said. "Now I have to go. Remember, you're just playing a part like an actress."

Callie ended the call before I could say anything else. I knew she was right, but I was still so nervous. I blamed the wine we drank the other night, three bottles of the stuff between the two of us, for me saying yes to this. I was always the straight-laced girl that played by the rules. I wasn't the sort of girl who dated for money. But Callie made being an escort sound pretty glamorous and if this deal was half as sweet as she had led me to believe it would be then I was all good. For years I had craved being able to drop the miss perfect persona and just be me. Maybe this was my chance to make it happen.

I checked my watch. Five minutes until we were due to meet. This moment was my last chance to back out of this if that's what I was going to do. But I wasn't going anywhere, and I knew it. One week, one hundred thousand dollars, no strings, and no sex stuff? I would have to be mad not to do it. And there was no law to say I had to use the word escort, right?

"Miss Rogers?" a deep male voice said from behind me.

I took a deep, calming breath and turned around and forced myself to smile despite my disappointment. The man behind me must have been almost sixty and although he looked clean and well groomed, he was nothing like my type at all.

And then I could see why this guy was paying for company. Not, as Callie told me because he wanted no strings and no mess, but because this guy would struggle to find a twenty-five-year fiancé that he wasn't paying. I felt as though I could already hear the judgement in his family's voices when I was introduced to them. He might as well just say this is Lena, my gold digger.

"That's me," I said, hoping I sounded happier than I felt.

"Please come with me," he said, returning my smile. "Your plane is almost ready for take-off. We just need to get your luggage loaded and you seated."

I followed him, pulling my suitcase behind me. He slowed down slightly and took my suitcase from me and then he fell into step beside me. I forced myself to keep looking straight ahead, not wanting him to catch me giving him the side eye and coming up disappointed.

"Alfred?" a shrill female voice called from behind us. He stopped walking.

"Sorry, please excuse me," he said.

Unsure what to do, I stopped and waited for him.

"When you have finished helping Miss Rogers, could you please go up to the second-floor lounge and take Mr Andrews' daughter to runway three," the woman asked.

"Sure," he said and then we were walking again, and I felt a flicker of relief inside of me.

"You work for the airport?" I asked.

"Of course," Alfred smiled. "Why else would I be escorting you to your plane?"

Why else indeed I thought. I wasn't about to admit I had no idea what the man I was meeting looked like and I had momentarily thought it was him. I thought quickly.

"I thought a member of the crew would come for me," I lied.

"Oh no, they will be doing all of their safety checks at this point," Alfred said.

We reached a door which Alfred pulled open and gestured for me to step through. I thanked him and I found myself outside. The client's private plane sat gleaming merely meters away.

"You can board whenever you are ready Ms Rogers. I'll

put your luggage in the hold. Would you prefer to keep your purse?" he asked.

"Yes, thank you," I said.

I walked to the plane on slightly unsteady legs. I told myself to calm down. There was still every chance Callie hadn't lied to me and this guy was hot. And if she had lied, I was just going to think of the money and smile and get on with it, just like I had when I had thought I was about to be seen as the latest gold digger in someone's family.

I climbed the steps to the plane and a flight attendant dressed in a crisp looking navy skirt and blazer over a white blouse smiled widely at me.

"Hi," I said.

"Good morning," she replied. "Welcome aboard. Mr Summers is waiting for you on the right. Enjoy your flight."

I kept my smile frozen in place, but I felt anything but happy. But no. I knew I was being paranoid. It couldn't be him … could it? But it was. As I stepped into the aisle, he stood up, his dark brown eyes blazing as he looked at me in undisguised anger.

"What the fuck are you doing here Lena?" he demanded.

RAFAEL

This had to be a fucking joke. When I had told Callie I wanted a professional for this week, I had meant it. And I was paying enough for the week to ensure that's what I should have gotten. If I had wanted an amateur, I would have pulled some girl in a club. But I wanted someone who would play their role without any fuss. And while I had no intention of having sex with the woman, part of the act would be us sharing a hotel room. And I couldn't see Lena being any happier with that arrangement than I was.

I looked at Lena, waiting for some sort of explanation, but she just stood there mute looking back at me. I couldn't help but notice that she was pretty. She had full red lips and full cheeks that made me want to reach out and touch them. Her little nose was a tiny bit too small for her face, but rather than spoil her looks, it added a slight vulnerability to her features that I liked. Her long, straight hair shone, the dark brown color of it making her green eyes stand out.

And her body. What could I say about her body? She had large breasts and curvy hips, the sort of hour glass figure a lot of women would kill for. I couldn't help but imagine my hands on those hips, her breasts in my mouth. She was dressed casually – jeans, flat black shoes, and a black t shirt – but that didn't make her look any less fuckable.

I cleared my throat, pushing the image away. It didn't matter how good this woman looked, there was no way I could spend a full week with her. She had always rubbed me up the wrong way. She was sarcastic and abrasive, always as cold as ice, and I got the impression she went out of her way to be cold to people on purpose. I could imagine her being some sort of trophy wife, the high maintenance type who pride themselves on being high maintenance and that wasn't something I found even remotely attractive.

"Well?" I demanded, when it became clear to me that Lena wasn't going to answer my question without further prompting. "What are you doing here? I wanted a professional."

Lena held her head up high and smiled at me, but the smile didn't reach her eyes.

"I am a professional," she said. "See my old boss was a complete wanker and he fired me so I had to find a new job quickly. And here we are."

"Yeah, this isn't going to work," I said.

Lena came towards me, some of the casual arrogance gone from her face.

"Look, I need the money, ok? And you need someone who can pretend to like you for a week. Who better than someone who's been doing exactly that for years at work," she said.

"But Lena, you were bad at it," I pointed out. "You think I don't know you didn't like me?"

"No, but you have no idea how much I dislike you. And that was me just doing enough to not openly despise you. It'll be different if I'm actually trying," she said.

"I don't think …" I started.

"Five minutes until take off," a voice said from behind me.

One of the cabin crew was approaching us. As she neared us, Lena reached out and picked a piece of imaginary fluff from my shoulder, a strangely intimate gesture. I was about to demand to know what she was doing when she smiled, and this time, the smile lit up her whole face and made her eyes sparkle.

"I can't wait to meet your family," Lena said. She clapped her hands in supposed joy. "Especially your sister. I never had a sister, and it will be nice to almost have one. And if she's anything like you, I just know I'm going to love her."

The cabin crew member stopped beside Lena and smiled.

"Would you like to get seated?" she said.

"Sure," Lena said. She looked down at me. "Are you moving over or am I taking the window seat?"

"There are like twelve other seats," I pointed out.

"Yes, but none of those are next to you," she said. She rolled her eyes and smiled at the cabin crew member. "Honestly. Who said romance is dead huh?"

"Ah but he's cute so that makes up for it," the cabin crew member laughed back.

I rolled my eyes and moved over. Lena sat down beside me and fastened her seat belt and then she took my hand in hers and absently rubbed her thumb over the back of my hand. I tried to ignore the way her hand felt in mine, the way my skin tingled where it touched hers. Shit. Maybe she was a professional after all.

"My name is Helen," the cabin crew member said. "Once we're in the air, if you need anything, just let me know. Otherwise, your meal and drinks will be served approximately twenty minutes after take-off. Is that ok?"

I nodded my head and she moved away, and I pulled my hand away from Lena's.

"What was that?" I asked.

"Call it an audition," she said. "And don't tell me it didn't work, because even you were buying it at one point when you told me there were other seats, not demanded I get off the plane."

I sighed. She had a point. She had drawn me into the role she was playing, and she had more than fooled Helen. But could she keep it up all week? I had very little choice but to let her try it. It was Lena or no one at this point.

"Fine. The job is yours. But one fuck up Lena, one person who suspects it's all a sham, and that's your fee gone," he said.

Lena considered this for a moment.

"Your grandmother," she said finally.

"What about her?" I said.

"If your grandmother suspects this is a sham, then you don't pay me. She's the one you care about and if I agree to just anyone suspecting something, all you have to do is come clean to a trusted friend and have them doubt us and boom, my pay is gone," she said.

I smiled despite myself.

"I like the way you're thinking Lena. Maybe this can work after all. You're on," I said.

I held my hand out and Lena shook it and again, I ignored the tingling sensation where our palms touched. It looked like we were about to do this for better or for worse.

* * *

I WAS ONCE MORE REGRETTING AGREEING to this. After Lena did her little show on the plane, she barely spoke another word to me. Don't get me wrong, I didn't particularly want to talk to her either, but I was concerned that she wasn't going to be able to put herself into this role completely. And it wasn't just on the plane that she ignored me. When we landed and got off the plane, she was all smiles and thank you to our driver who loaded the luggage into the trunk and held her door open for her, but I might as well not have been there. She still didn't speak a word to me.

My concerns were growing with each mile we drove, until finally, we pulled up at the hotel where all of the wedding events would be taking place. I had, by that point, pretty much decided to call the whole thing off. I opened my mouth to tell Lena that, but she was already on her way out of the car. I sighed and got out myself and before I had a chance to speak to Lena, my parents appeared in the doorway to the hotel. Wonderful.

They came towards us as the driver unloaded our luggage. My mom pulled me into a hug, and I hugged her back.

"Hi mom, how's things?" I said.

"Good," she smiled. "It's so nice to see you. And who is this?"

She released me and turned her focus to Lena. I swallowed hard. This was it. Lena was going to ruin this whole thing. Was she just going to come out and tell my mom I had paid her to be my girlfriend? Or was she going to be the moody bitch she had been all of the way here?

As it turned out, she was neither. She smiled, the one that lit up her whole face, and embraced my mom. They air kissed each other's cheeks and Lena acted like she had been doing that her whole life. Maybe she had. I wouldn't know.

"Mrs Summers," Lena gushed. "It's so nice to meet you. Rafael has told me so much about you. I'm Lena."

"Ah well then I am on the back foot," my mom said. She swatted at my arm. "Because Raf here has kept you all to himself. He has been all very mysterious. He wouldn't even tell me your name you know; he just said he was bringing his girlfriend and that I would like you."

"Well, I hope that much is true," Lena smiled. She

gestured down at herself. "And please don't think I thought this was an appropriate outfit in which to meet you. I thought we would have time to get to our room and change first."

"Nonsense," my mom exclaimed. "You look lovely. Doesn't she look lovely Harry?"

My dad, used to my mom's exuberance and happy to stay quiet for the most part, nodded his head and smiled.

"Yes," he agreed. "Nice to meet you, Lena."

"And you, Mr Summers," Lena said.

"Now no more of that Mr and Mrs Summers nonsense, you hear me?" my mom said. She linked her arm through Lena's and began to lead her inside. "I'm Sofia and this is Harry. Come along and grab a drink and meet the others. Harry, can you have a porter come and collect their luggage and get them checked in?"

"Oh no, I need to change first," Lena said.

"Nonsense," my mom said, her word of the day it seemed. "You look just fine. We're only going to have one quick drink in the bar."

Lena gave in graciously and allowed my mom to lead her away. I followed my mom and Lena down a corridor as my mom chatted away and asked Lena the occasional question which she answered fully and with interest. I found myself starting to relax a little bit. Lena was good at this, and if she wanted to turn off the charm and ignore me when we were alone, I could live with that. In fact, now I had seen her in action and knew she could turn it on and off like a tap, I would welcome it.

We reached the bar and my mom and Lena entered followed by me. There were a few people sitting at the tables, but overall, the bar was pretty quiet, and I instantly spotted the table my family were sitting at. There was my grand-mother and Sammy, my sister, and of course my niece, Eve.

Bradley, Sammy's husband to be wasn't there and I realized that his side of the family weren't there at all. It must have been some sort of a bride thing. I don't know. To be honest, I don't really care. I loved my sister, don't get me wrong, but I remembered when weddings lasted a day and that was more than enough. Now we have to be here for the week and get involved in all kinds of shit I would rather avoid having to do. Weddings weren't really my thing. Sue me.

The irritable feeling inside of me went away a lot when my grandmother got up from the table and came over to me. She pinched my cheeks which really should have embarrassed me and if it had been anyone else doing it, it would definitely have been embarrassing, but my grandmother could do pretty much anything to me and I would be cool with it.

"Darling boy," she said, smiling and pulling me in for a hug. "It's been too long. You know, one of these times, you'll leave me abandoned and when you come and see me, you'll find me dead."

"Don't be so melodramatic, Grandma," I said, laughing. "I only saw you last Tuesday. It's not even a week ago."

"I know," my grandmother agreed. "But you should have seen the look on that poppet's face when I was talking."

I realized she meant Lena and I had to admire the fact that my grandmother had almost given her another reason to hate me. My grandmother beckoned to Lena who stepped forward and smiled.

"It's a pleasure to meet you," Lena said.

"Ah, don't be so sure about that now," my grandmother said with a wink. "You might find I'm a cranky old thing."

"Well, that you are mother," my dad put in, joining us around the table. "But we love you anyway."

My grandmother shook a fist at my dad and then laughing, she hugged Lena. While they were hugging, my father gave me our key card for our room. I glanced at it. Room five nineteen.

"Welcome to the family dear," my grandma said, releasing Lena and smiling warmly at her. "You feel like one who might stick around."

I felt instantly guilty when she said that, but at the same time, I felt relieved that my plan seemed to be working. My grandmother was in her early nineties and while she seemed to be as fit as she had ever been, I knew how quickly someone that age could go downhill, and I wanted her to think I had someone. She had always dreamed of the day I met a nice girl and settled down and I wanted her to think I had done just that.

"That's the plan," Lena said, smiling at my grandmother.

"Grandma, this is Lena," I said. "Lena, my grandmother, Evelyn."

The two women smiled at each other again and then as my grandma returned to her seat, I introduced Lena and Sammy to each other. They smiled and exchanged pleasantries and then Eve surprised everyone by holding her arms up to Lena to be picked up. Lena didn't hesitate. She scooped Eve up and plonked her on her hip and began cooing over how cute she was.

"I can't believe it," Sammy said, shaking her head in wonder. "She's usually so clingy. She'll only go to us, Bradley, and his parents and that's about it. She won't even go to my best friend, her godmother, like that."

"You must be a natural," my mom said, smiling at Lena and pulling out a chair for her to sit down.

Lena sat down and thanked her, sitting Eve on her lap.

"Do you have children of your own Lena?" Sammy asked.

Lena shook her head.

"No," she said. "To be honest, I never really wanted children."

I cringed inside as my family all went quiet and then Sammy broke the silence.

"Oh, you and Raf might not be the best match then. He wants at least four don't you, big bro?" she said.

I didn't get a chance to respond before Lena laughed and nodded her head.

"Oh, believe me, he made it known it was a deal breaker. And I have to admit I've come around to the idea. I think before I always thought I didn't want children because I hadn't met anyone I could see as being a father to my children. Until I met Rafael."

She turned and smiled at me and squeezed my hand. I returned the smile, relieved that she had turned the situation around so effortlessly. She really was good at this. Maybe even better than Callie.

My dad went up to the bar and came back a few minutes later with an ice bucket and a bottle of champagne. The bar tender followed him with a tray full of champagne flutes. We all took a glass and the bar tender poured the drinks for us and then we toasted to Sammy and Bradley and the start of their life together.

The conversation flowed almost as quickly as the drinks and somewhere along the line, Bradley and his parents joined us and then Melissa, Sammy's best friend and her maid of honor and Liam, Bradley's best man. The other bridesmaids and groomsmen weren't there yet, and I silently wondered how the hell they had gotten out of it, and I hadn't.

I hadn't realized how late it had gotten until my mom announced that she was starving, and I saw that it was after nine o'clock. We decided no one really wanted to go and get changed at this point and so rather than go through to the restaurant, we ordered bar meals and stayed where we were. Once we finished eating our food, we were soon back to talking and laughing and at some point, Sammy excused herself so she could take Eve up to bed.

As evening became night, the lights in the bar dimmed down and a disco started up. I knew I must be drunk when Lena took my hand and pulled me to my feet.

"Let's dance," she said.

Normally I would have said no way, but somehow, I found myself following her onto the half full dance floor and soon we were laughing and dancing, twirling each other around and genuinely having fun. Or maybe it was only me that was genuinely having fun. Maybe Lena was playing her role all too well. Whatever. I was enjoying myself and I was sick of over thinking this, probably because I was on the drunk side of tipsy, and I was just going to let my hair down and have fun tonight. Everyone kept telling me that weddings were meant to be fun after all.

By the time the disco ended, and the lights came back up in the bar, I was pleasantly tired and a little bit breathless. Lena and I went back to our table and said our good nights to the others who were still finishing up their drinks and then we left the bar and headed for the elevator.

"We're in room number five nineteen," I said, and Lena hit the button for the fifth floor. "You know, I think my family might like you more than they like me."

"Well, who can blame them?" Lena giggled. "I'm just naturally likable."

"What? And you're saying I'm not?" I teased her.

"I'm saying you hide the nicer side of yourself much better than I do. How's that?" she said.

"Not great but I'll take it," I said with a laugh.

The elevator reached our floor, and we made our way down the hallway, counting off the other rooms as we went. Ours was about half way along the hallway and I got the key card out and opened the door. I pushed it wide open and indicated for Lena to go in first. She smiled her thanks at me and stepped into the room.

"Nice," she said, looking around.

The room was a fair size and in the centre was a large four poster bed with a small bedside cabinet on either side of it. Opposite the bed was a desk with a chair and on the wall above the desk, a huge flat screen TV. In the corner was a full length couch that didn't look like the most uncomfortable place to sleep. There was also a large wardrobe and a chest of drawers along the back wall on the other side of the bed, opposite the door.

Lena made her way through the room as I slipped the key card into the slot for electric and the lights pinged on. I closed and locked the door and watched as Lena opened the bathroom door and peered inside of it. I could see into the room over her shoulder. The bathroom wasn't huge, but it was more than adequate, and it had a decent sized shower and a separate bath tub. There was a double sink beneath the mirror and plenty of toiletries sat out on the side for us to use.

It wasn't exactly the most luxurious place I had ever been to, but it was nice enough for its purpose and as long as Sammy was happy with her wedding venue, who the hell was I to complain?

Lena came back out of the bathroom and opened up her suitcase. She pulled out a slinky looking red silk night dress and smiled at me.

"I won't be too long," she said, going into the bathroom.

I had to wait for her to come back lout before I could get settled on the couch because I needed to use the toilet and brush my teeth, so I began to unpack my suitcase while I waited. I didn't have to wait too long, although I had finished unpacking by the time Lena came back out of the bathroom. She took my breath away. She had removed her make up and brushed her hair out and while she looked good with her make up on and her hair done, I had to admit she looked just as beautiful natural.

And that night dress. Holy fuck. It sat mid-thigh on her, the material thin and shiny red. The straps were thin spaghetti straps and the neckline was edged with black lace. It hung just right on her hips, clinging to her curves and showing them off. Her nipples poked through the thin material, and I had to wonder why they were hard. It wasn't cold in the room.

"Wow," I said, unable to stop myself from reacting to the sight of her.

Lena laughed softly, her cheeks turning pink at my compliment. She turned her face down slightly and peered up at me through her long dark eyelashes.

"You like it?" she said.

That was one way of putting it. I nodded, not trusting myself to speak. Lena stepped away from the bathroom door and I stood up and cleared my throat. I started towards the bathroom and found myself face to face with Lena. She started to move to one side, and I went the same way. We both went the other way, and it was that moment where we should have both laughed at the awkwardness of it, but suddenly being this close to her wasn't awkward and there was nothing funny about the way my body was reacting to the sight of her.

Before I could talk myself out of it, I reached out, clasped my hand on the back of Lena's head and pulled her to me, pressing my lips against hers. She moaned into my mouth and pressed her body against mine. I could feel the cool silk of her night dress and the heat of her skin through my clothes. I worked my hand into her hair and the other hand rested on her ass for a moment before I moved it around to the front of her body.

I slid my hand up her thigh inner, underneath the silky material of her night dress and I found her already dripping wet slit. I pushed my fingers between her lips and found her pulsing clit with my fingers. I began to massage it, moving it back and forth and side to side and making Lena cry out. I deepened our kiss, interlocking my tongue with hers.

I needed to taste her, to touch her. I needed to fuck her. I wanted to feel that hot, wet little pussy tight around my hard cock. I pulled my mouth from hers and kissed down her neck and across her exposed shoulder. I grabbed the hem of her night gown with one hand and tugged it up. Lena took the hint and pulled it off over her head, dropping it on the ground beside us. I kept working her clit as I kissed down her chest and then I sucked one of her nipples into my mouth.

As I worked her, she reached towards me and fumbled my belt open and then she pushed her hand inside of my boxer shorts and before I knew it, her fist was wrapped around my cock. She moved her fist up and down, her pace matching the pace I was using on her. She took my breath away and I had to release her breast to take a gulp of air before I found myself suffocating.

It didn't matter. She was already so close to climax that one more hard press on her clit took her over the edge. For a moment, her hand stopped moving up and down on me and instead, she gripped my cock tightly as her head went back and the tendons on her neck stood out, She moaned my name as a shudder went through her body and then she lifted her head back up and looked at me.

Her pupils were dilated with lust as she looked at me and her lips were pink and swollen from our passionate kissing. Her chest moved as she panted for breath, but like an expert, she was already working me again and I knew if I didn't pull her hand away from me soon, this would be over before it had really begun.

I grabbed Lena's wrist and slipped her hand back out of my boxer shorts. I kissed her again and started to walk her over to the bed, shedding my clothes as we went. We reached the bed, and I pushed Lena backwards onto it. She fell onto the bed on her back, right where I wanted her.

I quickly pulled off my socks and shoes, the only things I was still left wearing. I clambered onto the bed and Lena scooted back to make room for me. She opened her legs wide, and I could see the moisture on her slit and at the opening of her pussy and I moaned at the sight of her open to me and inviting me inside of her. I knelt between her legs and lowered myself down on top of her and then I lined my cock up with her pussy. In one long stroke, I entered Lena and filled her up.

She gasped as I slammed into her, and her hands came up and wrapped around my shoulders. I began to thrust inside of her, slowly at first, enjoying the warm tightness of her against me. We kissed as I moved inside of her and her hands roamed freely over my back and sides, then they went down to my ass and she clutched at my ass cheeks, pushing me in deeper and deeper until I was all of the way inside of her.

She let me keep moving for a second longer and then she bucked her hips, taking me unawares and we rolled to the side and then Lena came up on top of me. What a sight she was as she started to move, and her breasts bounced wildly up and down in time with her thrusts.

Her skin had a light sheen of sweat on it making it look like she was almost iridescent in the moonlight that came in through the still open curtains. Her hair whipped around her face as she worked us both up into a frenzy. She ran one hand down her flat stomach and then she pushed her fingers between her lips, touching herself as she rode me.

I watched the show, my breath catching in my throat. God she was fucking hot. So, fucking hot. I couldn't stand it any longer and although I had planned to wait until Lena climaxed, it was my turn to buck my hips and throw Lena to the side. I got back on top of her, and I began to up the pace of my thrusts, moving my hips faster and faster, giving her no reprieve. She clung to me, panting and gasping and as a rush of warm liquid flooded out of her, she pressed her face against my shoulder and made a sound that was almost a whimper. She dug her nails into my back and held on as though she might float away if she let go of me.

As her orgasm ripped through her body, her pussy clenched even more tightly around me and that did it for me. I felt the heat in my cock and in my stomach and then I was climaxing, pleasure zipping around my body and sending me to places I didn't even know existed.

My cock gave one final spasm, and I was done, the pleasure more intense than anything I had ever felt before. I slipped out of Lena and rolled to the side and we lay that way, side by side, as we panted for air. I couldn't believe that this woman, by far the most annoying woman I had ever met, had also turned out to be by far the best sex I had ever had. There was some sort of irony there. There had to be.

When we finally recovered, I got up and went to use the bathroom like I had planned to earlier.

I did what I had to do and then I came back into the main room and Lena was laid where I left her, fast asleep. She was laid on her back, her head turned towards me, and she had one hand on the pillow beside her face. She looked peaceful, almost angelic, with her eyes closed and her lips slightly parted. Her skin was covered in goose bumps, and I could feel a bit of a chill kin the air myself now.

I didn't want Lena to freeze in the night, so I gently moved the duvet from beneath her and put it over her instead. She muttered something I couldn't understand and then she gave a quiet snore and then her breathing evened out again. I smiled down at her. After we had sex, I had planned to sleep in the bed with Lena, but now she had fallen asleep while I was gone, it felt wrong somehow, and reluctantly, I went to the wardrobe and got out the spare pillow and blanket and I went and laid down on the couch.

LENA

$\mathcal{I}$ woke up slowly, clawing my way out of a lovely deep, restful sleep. I rubbed my hand over my eyes and yawned. My memory came rushing back to me and I remembered having sex with Rafael. It was the last thing I had planned on doing, but I remembered that in the moment, it had felt so right. He had been nothing but nice and attentive to me all night and while I knew it was an act, I couldn't help but feel attracted to him, and when he kissed me, honestly, I just thought why not?

He wasn't in the bed beside me and I looked around expecting to see him getting dressed, or maybe seeing the bathroom door closed while he was showering. But no. He was asleep on the couch where he had obviously spent the night. He must have gotten back out of the bed after I fell asleep.

I wasn't entirely sure how I felt about any of this, but Rafael being on the couch and not in the bed with me told me exactly how he felt about it. He regretted it. That was ok. I could say I did too, we made a mistake, blah blah blah, and then we could just put it behind us.

My decision made, I slipped out of bed, conscious of the fact that Rafael could wake up at any moment and I was naked. It was probably stupid after last night, but I couldn't help but feel that way now he had chosen not to sleep in the bed with me.

I went into the bathroom and got a large fluffy white towel and wrapped myself in it, and then I went back to the bedroom. I sorted through my suitcase and found the white three quarter length pants and yellow vest top I wanted to wear that day. I found underwear and my toiletries bag and then I went into the bathroom.

I showered and washed my hair and then I brushed my teeth and I dried myself off and got dressed. I gathered up my dirty clothes from the night before and I went back into the bedroom.

"Morning," Rafael said.

He was still on the couch, but he was sitting up, the blanket folded up beside him. He was wearing a pair of white boxer shorts and nothing else and instantly I remembered the way his skin had felt on mine, the way he had moved inside of me and made me come so hard I had feared I would pass out.

"Good morning," I said as casually as possible.

I turned my back to Rafael. Seeing his naked, muscular chest was bad for my resolve. I began to unpack my clothes and hang them up in the wardrobe with his, more so that I had a reason to have my back to him without being rude than for any real urge to not live out of my suitcase.

I had moved on to putting my underwear in one of the drawers when Rafael spoke up behind me.

"So about last night," he said. He sounded like he didn't really know what to say next, but I had no idea what to say and I hadn't been the one to bring it up, so I wasn't about to bail him out. Instead, I made a hmm sound and waited for him to go on. "I … Well, I wanted to apologize. I don't know what came over me. The drinking, the dancing, and that night dress you were wearing … Yeah. I shouldn't have acted on the way I felt though."

I shrugged my shoulders and finally turned to look at him.

"It wasn't exactly one sided. We both drank a bit too much and well, shit happens right," I said with a smile.

"Right," Rafael confirmed. "So, what now? We just act like it never happened and get on with the rest of the week?"

"Yes," I said. "And we keep it professional from now on."

"Agreed," Rafael said. He looked like he was going to say something else but then he gave his head a small shake and when he did speak, I felt like it wasn't whatever he had been planning on saying. "I'm going to quickly get showered and dressed and then should we go and have some breakfast? I'm starving."

I opened my mouth to say yes, but my stomach chose that moment to growl and instead, we both laughed.

"I think that's answer enough," I said as Rafael headed for the bathroom, and I sat down at the desk to put some make up on. That hadn't gone half as badly as I had expected it to.

* * *

"OH WOW THAT'S AMAZING," I moaned as I swallowed my bite of bacon sandwich.

The bread was fresh and soft, and the bacon was cooked to perfection, crispy and salty and delicious. Evelyn smiled at me over the top of her tea cup. She sipped her tea and then she laughed softly.

"You know, that reminds me of something from when Rafael was just a boy," she said.

"Oh no, don't Grandma," Rafael said, but he was laughing indulgently and we all knew she was going to tell the story and he wasn't going to object to it any more than he already had.

"Rafael always loved bacon when he was small. He would have had it for breakfast, lunch and dinner if his parents would have let him," Evelyn said. "Well one day, we took him and Sammy on a day out to a working farm where they had animals you could pet and feed and you could look around at all of the equipment and what not. Raf fell in love with this little piglet named Shirley and when it was time it leave, he cried because he had to leave her. Anyway, he got over it and as far as we knew, that was that.

"But nope. A few months later when we had all but forgotten about Shirley, Rafael came home from day care crying. He was inconsolable and he wouldn't tell anyone what was wrong. Eventually, his mom got it out of him though. He had learned where bacon came from and of course that made him think of Shirley and the fact that someone would one day eat her. He swore off bacon that day and it was a good two or three years before he wanted any again. My husband was alive then, and he asked Rafael what had changed his mind and do you know what he said? As serious as the day is long he looks at his grandpa and shrugs his shoulders and says Shirley will be long eaten now. I don't care about the other pigs."

Rafael and I laughed along with her. She really was entertaining and the way she told her story only made it better. She knew just when to pause and when to carry on. She smiled when she saw she was making us laugh and I decided to take full advantage of this situation, while still playing my part of the good girlfriend.

"Do you have any more stories about Rafael?" I asked. "The more embarrassing the better."

"There was the time when he got completely obsessed with his little willy," Evelyn said with a wicked glow on her cheeks as she grinned.

"Oh, Grandma no, not that one," Rafael said.

"Shush now," Evelyn said. She looked at me. "You want to hear it right?"

"Absolutely," I said.

Rafael stood up and at first, I thought he was leaving in anger, but I saw he was smiling and shaking his head.

"I can't talk you out of it, but I don't need to hear it. I'm going to go and get you another pot of tea Grandma," he said.

As Rafael walked away, Evelyn grinned at me.

"He wasn't even three when it started. It was like he just sort of discovered his willy one morning and once he knew about it, he had to be touching it. Like all of the time. And not through his clothes might I add," Evelyn said. We both laughed at the last part and then Evelyn carried on. "Now that was bad at home, but it was even worse at day care. Harry and Sofia got called in for a meeting with day care centre manager and they went along wondering what was so serious they both had to be present for it.

"Well they got there and the manager explained to them that Rafael had gotten into the habit of pulling down his pants and his underwear and holding his willy. Not playing with it per se, just … holding it," Evelyn said.

I shrieked with laughter, unable to stop myself from picturing it. Tears streamed down my face and Evelyn nodded her head.

"That's pretty much the reaction Harry and Sofia had, but the day care centre manager didn't find it very funny at all and she informed them that Rafael was no longer welcome at the day care centre," Evelyn said.

"And now Grandma likes to tell people that I once got thrown out of a day care centre for touching my willy,"

Rafael added, sitting back down with a fresh pot of tea for Evelyn. "With no context, you can imagine the horrified silence that follows that statement."

I was laughing so hard I was in danger of snorting, but I reeled myself in slightly. Evelyn nodded her agreement to Rafael's statement.

"You have no idea how much fun it is to do that," Evelyn said. "Once I explain it's always alright. They think it's just because I'm old that I worded it badly. I don't want to disappoint any one so I let them think they're right. But we know differently don't we Rafael?"

Rafael made a grunting sound which could have meant anything but Evelyn seemed content enough to take it as agreement. Rafael poured her a fresh cup of tea and added a splash of milk.

"Be careful," he said when she reached for it. "Remember it's fresh so it'll be hot."

Evelyn patted his lower arm and smiled at him and then at me.

"He's a good boy," she said. "But you know that already don't you dear?"

I smiled and nodded my head. I could hardly do anything else in my role.

"Stop it, you're embarrassing me," Rafael said, but I could see he was trying not to smile at her praise.

He really did seem to think the world of the old lady and when he was with her, it was like a different side to him came out. He was caring and gentle and attentive. The more I saw of him interacting with Evelyn, the more I saw that sweet side of him, and I was starting to think that maybe there was more to him than I had thought. Maybe the cold hard exterior was just an act put on in the office to stop anyone thinking he was too soft. Maybe outside of the office, he was this genuinely nice person.

Stop it, I told myself. Don't even start to go there.

Having sex with Rafael was one thing, because there was no denying that he was hot as hell. But actually liking him? Ugh no.

RAFAEL

I sat and looked out of the restaurant window while I waited for Lena. It looked like a decent enough day out there, and I wondered if maybe Lena and I should go for a walk around the grounds after lunch. While it was nice to have her be nice to me, sometimes it was hard to remember what was real and what wasn't and I figured a bit of time alone would remove the blurred lines and make me remember what I hated about her. Ok, hate was maybe a bit strong. Perhaps actively disliked was better.

Despite my dislike for Lena, I didn't regret having sex with her the other night. Was that weird? Maybe it was. But the fact of the matter was that we were two consenting adults and like her or not, there is no denying that Lena was fucking hot. I don't think I would be human if I didn't want to have sex with her.

I pretended to think it was a mistake the morning after it because Lena seemed to feel like it was a mistake for her, and I figured it would make things less complicated if I said I regretted it too and we would keep things business like from now on than it would if I had spoken the truth instead and said that I didn't regret it one bit and I would in fact be open to doing that again.

It was funny because before I saw her in that nightdress, I had never imagined myself having sex with her. Not really. I knew she was attractive, but in my mind, that didn't excuse the way she was always so cold to me and the way she always spoke to me with a level of derision in her voice. Really it was beyond me how anyone liked her when she wasn't acting.

Even now, she was disrespecting me, and I was paying her to do the opposite. I had had some work related calls to make this morning, so I had arranged to meet Lena for lunch here in the restaurant and she was meant to have been here five minutes ago. I knew it wasn't that long, but it wasn't like she had anything else to do and even if there was a genuine reason, would it have killed her to do the polite thing and let me know she was going to be late?

I could feel myself getting more and more annoyed the longer I sat there and I checked my watch again and saw that ten minutes had passed since the time we were due to meet. Fuck that. I got up and left the restaurant and headed back towards the elevators. I would go and get on with some more work and Lena did eventually decide to breeze into the restaurant, she wouldn't find me there waiting for her like an idiot.

As I stormed down the hallway, I realized that I could hear Lena's voice. I looked around in annoyance wondering where she was, but I couldn't see her. For me to be able to hear her but not see her while I was in this spot, she had to be in the bar. That got my back even further up. She was sitting drinking instead of meeting me. Great.

I knew an argument in public wouldn't be a good look for

the façade I was presenting, but I couldn't let Lena just take the piss out of me and not say anything. This was unacceptable and I intended to nip it in the bud right now. I approached the bar but as I go to the door, I saw that Lena wasn't actually drinking. She was sitting with Sammy, the table in front of them empty except for Eve's sippy cup.

Sammy was crying and Lena had an arm around her talking to her. I knew I should move away, but I stayed in place, wondering what was going on. I soon got the gist of the conversation. Sammy was upset about the wedding. It sounded like she was having cold feet. Lena was calming her down, making her see that she loved Bradley and she did want to be his wife, that it was perfectly normal to have a freak out so close to the wedding. At the same time, she moved her hand, making shadow ducks, rabbits and more on the wall keeping Eve amused.

Eve sat happily on Lena's lap giggling in delight at the shadow creatures. Seeing Lena like that comforting my sister and entertaining my niece softened me slightly. Sammy being in floods of tears probably was more important than our lunch arrangements. I was still a bit pissed off that she hadn't even bothered to let me know though.

I decided to still head up to the room and when Lena text to see where I was when she eventually went to the restaurant to find me, I would come back down and forgive her for being late but make it clear she was to communicate with me in the future if something came up.

I was half way to the elevator when my cell phone pinged in my pocket. Great. That was likely more work calls I would have to make. As much as I would have liked to switch the damned thing off, the world didn't stop turning because of a wedding and that meant my business didn't stop running and that in turn meant I needed to be available, although I did have a good manager in place who easily handled the day to day stuff and most of the other stuff too. I couldn't complain really.

I frowned when I saw the ping sound hadn't indicated a voice message from a client or the manager, but instead, my cell phone showed a text message from Lena. I opened it and read it. It was short and to the point.

"I'm so sorry. I'm running late. I'll be as quick as I can. Feel free to eat without me and I'll grab something later if you need to get going. L x"

I read the message and then I saw the time stamp. The message had been sent twenty minutes before Lena and I were due to meet. So not only was she consoling my sister and taking care of me niece, she had also done the right thing and my lack of signal was the problem rather than her supposed lack of manners.

Feeling somewhat sheepish, I turned around and went back to the restaurant. I went back to the same table. I had barely gotten seated when a rather flustered looking Lena burst in. She saw me and hurried over to the table and sat down.

"I'm sorry," she said.

"It's ok," I told her. "What happened? How come you're late?"

Of course I already knew the answer to those questions, but in Lena's mind I didn't know where she had been and it would look weird not to ask.

"I was just helping Sammy with some wedding stuff," Lena said. "Stuff that would likely bore you, and time just kind of ran away with me."

I smiled and nodded, silently giving Lena another brownie point for not gossiping and protecting Sammy's moment of weakness.

"Should we order? I'm so hungry," Lena said, picking up a menu.

I nodded and picked up my menu too. Earlier, I had wondered why people liked Lena at all. I was starting to see why now. When she wasn't around me, she seemed to shed that cold exterior and open up a little bit and it made sense that people would like that version of her. Hell, I probably would have liked that version of her.

We ordered our lunch – a tuna salad for me and a jacket potato with cheese for her – and we chatted while we waited for it to come.

"Sammy mentioned something last night about taking a year out and traveling around Europe," Lena said. "Did you do that too?"

I shook my head.

"No," I said. "Sammy is a graphic designer, which means she can work from pretty much anywhere with an internet connection. She did do a year's travel, but she was building her business the whole time. Me, I chose a business selling sportswear wholesale, and well, I can't really do that unless I'm on site, so I didn't do the traveling thing."

"Couldn't your parents have hired a manager or something for a year if they wanted out before you were quite ready to take over?" she asked.

"It wasn't my parents' business," I told her. "I built my company from the ground up."

"Oh, I'm sorry," Lena said. "I always thought you inherited your father's business."

I shook my head again and I was about to tell her about my father's line of work when the waiter arrived with our food. We both thanked him, and we got tucked in to our food. We were chatting through the meal, not about anything in particular, just chit chat really. Lena told me she hadn't had a gap year either, but she had gone to Thailand for six weeks over the summer holidays before starting college. She was telling me about some of the things she saw, some of the places she had been. Her face was alight with her memories, and she talked so passionately about the place.

I couldn't help but smile at how enthusiastic she was, and for a moment there, it was hard to remember why I had always thought Lena was cold.

LENA

It was the night before the wedding. We had been to the rehearsal dinner – a huge affair with seven courses which had left me stuffed to bursting which wasn't good in the dress I was wearing – and then we had come to the bar and spent the evening drinking and having fun. Slowly, everyone had begun to leave because no one wanted to be ill throughout the wedding, but Rafael and I had hung back and now we were the only two people from our party still left in the bar.

It was a lot quieter than it had been on our first night here – there was no disco, just some soft music playing in the back ground and we actually had to have a conversation. Normally with Rafael and I that would have degenerated into a bitching session and then an argument, but tonight, it was different, we were different. We talked like civilized adults who actually might – shock horror – like each other.

For once, I wasn't acting the part of interested girlfriend when Rafael spoke. I was just being me, and I found that I was interested in what he had to say. He seemed to be equally attentive when I was speaking, and I didn't think it was an act. There was no one around to put the act on for, and while I had to take his lead, he was paying for the service. He could just tell me to be quiet, no one was around, we didn't need to do this. But he didn't.

"So, what will happen when your father retires?" I asked after Rafael mentioned the hours he was putting into his business.

"What do you mean what will happen? He'll stay home. Maybe take my mom on a cruise or something," Rafael said.

If he had been acting like his usual self, I would have said he was being sarcastic, but I really didn't think he was. I thought he had just missed the point of my questions.

"I meant with his business," I clarified. "Will you run it alongside your business, or will Sammy run it with hers? Or will he just sell it?"

"My father doesn't have a business," he replied. I looked at him, frowning in confusion and he smiled. "You've read one of those stupid articles haven't you about how I'm a billionaire bachelor and you assumed I made my money off my parents."

I nodded my head. There was no point in denying it. My line of questioning had made it obvious that's what I thought.

"Well firstly, I'm not quite a billionaire. A multi-millionaire sure, but not quite a billionaire. I suppose I could have been if I was greedy with my money but I'm not. My business is completely my own. I started it when I left college. I timed it just right. You could say I fell lucky. I am cool with that. But I worked my ass off too. And every penny I have, I have earned myself," Rafael said. "My father didn't have a business. He worked as a mechanic for a garage just down the road from the house we lived in when I was growing up and my mom worked as a cashier in a seven eleven. Some weeks, there was enough money, some weeks there wasn't. Sammy and I never went without though."

"I have to admit I am shocked," I said. "I „, I always assumed ..."

I tailed off, not sure how to end the sentence. Rafael smiled.

"You thought I was a spoilt brat who had grown up with a silver spoon in his mouth and then been given daddy's company to play at running while the board did all of the hard work," he said. "Right?"

"Almost right," I admitted. "I never thought you didn't work hard though. I just always thought you were doing it to make some sort of point to your father or whatever."

Rafael laughed and shook his head.

"Nope. I was doing it because like I said, growing up, some weeks, there wasn't enough money. But it wasn't until I was an adult and looking back on my childhood that I saw that. My parents never ever let Sammy and I know when they were struggling. They went without stuff, but we never did. And from the moment I worked that out, I vowed I was going to do everything I could to make them proud of me, and more than that, I vowed I was going to work hard enough so that there was never another week where there wasn't enough money for my parents," he said. "After I had worked for a few years, I was able to pay off their mortgage and do a few other things for them. They don't like to accept things from me, but I tend to leave them with no choice."

"It sounds like they're lucky to have you," I said.

"No, I'm the lucky one to have them as parents," Rafael said. He drained his glass and stood up. "Same again?"

I nodded my head and watched as Rafael headed up to the bar. I was really starting to see just how wrong I had been about him. He wasn't some silver spoon brat. He was a hard worker who loved his family and who just wanted to show them how much he appreciated them.

He was actually quite sweet. The second I thought that and didn't immediately try to discredit it, was the second that I knew that I was in trouble.

RAFAEL

I was surprised when Lena started taking such an interest in me. She actually seemed genuinely surprised to learn that I had worked for everything I have and she seemed moved when she learned that I made sure my parents were looked after. I also made sure my grandmother was looked after and I gave a ton of money to charity too but I didn't want Lena to think I was just blowing my own trumpet by pointing all of that out.

There was no need for Lena to be putting the act on because there was only me and her there from our group and other times when it had been just the two of us, she hadn't bothered with the act. So that meant I had to believe, no matter how far fetched it seemed, that Lena wasn't all bad. In fact, when she let her guard down a little bit, she was actually quite a nice person. This reminded me of my earlier thought about how she had always seemed to be cold to me, even before she had time to know she didn't like me and I decided that while things were going well, I was going to ask her about that.

I went back to the table with our drinks, and I sat down. I gave Lena her drink and she thanked me. I held my glass up.

"To old enemies becoming new friends," I said, hoping I hadn't read the situation wrong after all, because if I had, I was going to look awfully stupid with that toast.

Lena smiled and clinked her glass against mine.

"To old enemies becoming new friends," she repeated and then she smiled at me again and took a drink from her glass.

"So, you've asked me loads of questions about me and my life tonight. Let me ask you one," I said.

Lena nodded for me to go on.

"When I first met you, I thought you were one of those trophy wife type women. Hot but miserable, like the idea of smiling would make your face crack and you would marry someone hot and rich and you would both live unhappily ever after," I said.

"Oh my God no," Lena said, laughing. "That couldn't be further from the truth. I would much rather be single than in an unhappy relationship."

"Well, I have started to think that I might have been wrong about you. I've saw the mask slip a few times this week and underneath it all, you're not as much of an ice queen as you'd like me to believe you are. So, here's my question; why are you so cold and unapproachable with me? And don't say it's because you don't like me because you were like that before you had a chance to get me know enough to know whether or not you liked me," I said.

"I wouldn't say I was cold to you," Lena said but she looked away, refusing to meet my eyes as she said it.

"Right," I said. "And I suppose the chill blains I used to get in the office whenever you looked at me weren't because of you then huh?"

Lena snorted out a short laugh but then she shook her head, and she did look at me when she spoke again.

"It's nothing personal," she said. "It's not just you I keep at arm's length. Other than my immediate family and Callie, who has been my best friend since as long as I can remember, I don't let anyone get close and I find if I am nice to people, they want to get close. So, I am cold. Civil, polite, but cold."

"But why Lena? I don't get it. You're a nice person when you let yourself be. Why don't you want people to like you?" I asked her.

"It's not so much that I don't want people to like me. I have just accepted that a side effect of being cold and civil is that most people don't like you. I made my peace with it but it's not really my end goal," Lena said.

"So, what is your end goal?" I asked, well and truly confused now.

"I don't want to let anyone get close because I don't want to become dependent on anyone. I don't want to like anyone enough that them not being around anymore will bother me," she said.

"Oh Lena," I said. "Isn't that an awfully lonely way to live?"

She shrugged her shoulders.

"I suppose in a way it is yeah, but it's better than the alternative," she said.

"What? Having friends and people who care about you?" I pushed her.

"No. It's … not like that," she said. She sighed and carried on talking without me having to push her this time. "A good few years ago, I met who I thought was the love of my life, my soul mate, whatever you want to call it. We were so happy together. Everything was amazing. I should have known it was too good to be true."

She paused and I saw the unshed tears shining in her eyes. I was interested in where this was going but at the same time, I hadn't meant to upset her, and I was starting to regret asking her about this.

"I … He was my whole world and then he died in a car accident and I have never felt pain like it. I genuinely don't know how I got through it. But I know that I could never ever live through pain like that again. And the best way to make sure I never have to is to never get close enough to anyone to care one way or the other about them," she said.

I moved to the seat beside hers and took her hand in mine and squeezed it.

"I'm so sorry Lena," I said. "I can't imagine what that must have been like for you, especially when you were so young."

She sniffed and tried to smile but her bottom lip wobbled slightly, and she picked her drink up and took a big gulp from it to hide her pain. It didn't work. I could see her pain as clearly as if it was written in the air between us.

"I don't mean this to sound rude, and feel free to tell me to mind my own business, but do you really think that's what you're doing is a healthy way to cope with your grief? I mean have you considered therapy or something instead?" I asked.

Lena laughed at that, and I relaxed slightly. I could see beneath the laughter she was still upset but she didn't look quite as devastated as she had only seconds ago.

"I thought I was handling it the best way I could and for a long time, that was true. It was working for me, but now, well now not so much," she said.

"And why's that?" I asked.

She gave me another sad smile.

"Because I met someone who managed to get over the wall," she said.

A fat tear spilled from her eye as she said it and I reached up and used my thumb to wipe it away from her cheek. She looked at me as I touched her, and I looked back and then our lips were on each other's, and we were kissing.

While there was passion in the way we held each other as we kissed, the kiss itself was filled with more than just lust. It was deep and passionate, but it was also tender and full of emotion. When we broke apart, I could see the surprise I felt mirrored back to me on Lena's face.

"I'm not going anywhere, Lena," I said, my voice coming out low and husky.

She didn't reply. She just stood up, took my hand, and led me back to our room. I had a feeling that whatever happened next, I wouldn't be spending the night on the couch.

When Craig died, he took a part of me with him and the parts he left behind, he left them red, raw and gaping open. I felt the pain in every nerve of my body. I felt as though I was drowning, and I would never quite die but I would never be saved either.

Over the years, the pain of missing Craig had gotten easier to bare. But still, I had always been so careful not to let anyone in. And then there was Rafael. The one person I didn't really think I had to worry too much about keeping at arm's length because I didn't like him. Well that was a joke wasn't it. Because apparently, I liked him just fine now and somehow, I had let the bastard in and I was scared and excited all at the same time and I didn't know if I could even think clearly, let alone speak.

It was why I didn't attempt to answer Rafael when he said he wasn't going anywhere. That was by far the best thing he could have said in that moment, but I had nothing to give him back, at least not verbally. I needed to feel him close to me, his heart beating against my chest, his cock inside of me. I needed us to become one. I needed to let the last remaining bricks crumble away and I needed to finally let go of the last piece of the pain and torment I was forever holding onto.

I led Rafael into our hotel room and as I stepped inside, I was already pulling my clothes off. I turned back to Rafael and nodded for him to do the same. He didn't need telling twice and within less than a minute, we were both naked. We stood and faced each other, and I was already panting for breath with the effect Rafael was having on me. I thought he might be feeling the same way too because his chest was rising and falling much more quickly than usual.

I ran my eyes over his body taking in his muscular chest, his gorgeous abs, and of course his huge cock. I couldn't wait much longer to have him inside of me, and I closed the gap between us and wrapped my arms around Rafael's shoulders. I pulled him down to me and we kissed and he wrapped his arms around my waist.

He ran his hands down my body and onto my ass and he cupped it and lifted me off the ground. I wrapped my legs around his waist as his hands roamed back up my body and our tongues collided as we explored each other's mouths.

As we kissed, Rafael walked towards the bathroom. At first, I thought he was planning on us sharing a bath or a shower, but I was wrong. Instead, he kicked the bathroom door shut with us still in the bedroom and then he slammed me up against it and pressed himself against me. Fire flooded me as I felt him against every part of me.

He held me in place with his body and he ran his hands along my arms until he held my hands in his. He lifted my arms above my head and grasped both of my wrists with one of his hands and held them there.

He eased my feet back to the floor and with his free hand, he pushed my thighs apart. I side stepped eagerly with one foot, giving him all of the access he needed. He ran his fingers from my pussy to my clit, spreading a trail of juices as he went. I was already dripping wet for him and his gentle, teasing touch just made me wetter.

He smiled as I moaned in frustration and then he leaned his head down towards mine, but he even denied me his kiss, opting instead to lightly run his tongue over my lips. My whole body was thrumming with the need for more and he wasn't giving it to me. He was bringing me onto the edge and leaving me hanging, leaving me needing more.

I tried to writhe against his fingers, to press my clit against them but he smiled and shook his head and moved them away from me. I begged him to touch me, and he smiled again and brought his fingers back to me, but he only did the light, teasing touch again. I tried to get my hands free, but he had them held tightly enough that I couldn't do it.

I was just going to have to accept my situation and try to enjoy the ride. I closed my eyes and then I opened them again when he bit down on my nipple. I breathed in through my teeth as the stinging pain met the pleasure thrumming in my lower body and the two sensations accentuated each other, driving me even more mad.

When Rafael seemed to intuit that I couldn't take much more, he began to rub my clit faster and with more pressure. I moaned and when I writhed against his hand this time, he didn't pull his fingers away from me. Instead, he pushed his fingers back through my slit, and penetrated my pussy with them, leaving his thumb to tend to my clit's needs as he pushed his fingers in and out of me, rubbing them over my g spot with each movement.

The double stimulation pushed me closer and closer to my climax and I could feel it building up in both my stomach and in my clit. I was desperate for release and Rafael seemed to want to keep teasing me.

I felt him starting to pull his hand away, but I couldn't let him do that. Not this time. I thought that I would go insane if

I didn't get some relief soon. I clamped my thighs together tightly, trapping his hand there and I moved my hips so that my clit was rubbing over his thumb. I squatted down ever so slightly to get more pressure on my clit and Rafael did nothing to stop me.

I glanced at him, and he was looking back at me, his mouth slightly open. He smiled when I met his eye.

"You're amazing," he said, and then I was no longer fighting him.

He was pressing his thumb against my clit harder and faster, and my climax tore through me. I screamed Rafael's name as every nerve in my body throbbed to life and every bit of my skin tingled and pulsed. My clit throbbed, my pussy clenched, and my stomach contracted. I felt like my whole body was just a giant pulsing nerve ending that was so over whelmed with pleasure it didn't know quite what to do with itself. Just when I thought I couldn't take anymore, another wave of pleasure crashed over me, and I flooded Rafael's hand and the tops of my thighs with my juices.

My body shuddered as I came hard. I felt my eyes roll back in my head as I became consumed by pleasure. My vision went red, a throbbing, pulsing red that matched the way my body felt. I floated in ecstasy for a moment and then my eyes rolled back down and the red was gone and Rafael was back in my line of vision My knees buckled and if it wasn't for Rafael's body against mine, I know I would have collapsed onto the ground as all of my muscles turned to shaking, sated jelly.

Rafael stopped me from falling, but he gave me no respite. He released my arms and they flopped down across his shoulders and then he lifted me up again and pushed himself inside of me. I cried out as he filled me, rubbing over my still throbbing g spot.

I started to come back to myself as Rafael pounded into

me and I began to move in time to his rhythm. My movements seemed to spur him on and his breathing became more ragged with each thrust as he tried to hold himself back from orgasming.

He lost his fight, and he pressed me up against the door, holding me still as he spurted inside of me. I felt his cock twitching inside of my pussy and he whispered my name into my ear, his voice dripping with sex. It sent a shiver all through my body. I held him tightly as his body went rigid and he made a pained moan and then he relaxed and slid out of me and he took a step backwards and then carried me to the bed. He pulled the duvet back and laid me on the mattress and then he went around to the other side and lifted the duvet and raised a questioning eyebrow.

"I'm pretty sure it's ok," I said with a laugh.

He slid into the bed beside me, and I rolled to face him. We laid wrapped in each other's arms, looking into each other's eyes.

"No regrets?" Rafael said.

"No regrets," I agreed.

LENA

TWO WEEKS LATER

I smiled to myself as I walked to the store. My plan was to get everything I needed for dinner and then go to Rafael's office to wait for him to finish work so I could catch a ride back with him. I didn't mind the walk to the store – I enjoyed it in fact, but I hated walking back laden down with groceries.

I was shocked to discover that I was already missing Rafael. We had only been dating for two weeks, but we had seen each other pretty much every night of those short weeks. Last night was an exception because he had a conference call with someone in another time zone so he was at the office until the middle of the night. One night without seeing him and I was missing him this much already. That thought should have scared me, and it did a bit, but more than anything, I felt excited. I really felt like this could be the start of something special and I knew in my hearty, despite the pangs of guilt I occasionally felt that this was the right time to let Craig go.

I wandered into the store, debating what to cook for dinner. I went to the ATM to check my balance. That would decide to an extent what I could afford to buy. I was still between jobs, but I had an offer from a firm that I was seriously considering taking.

I put my card in and my jaw almost hit the ground when I saw my balance. What the fuck was that? The bank must have made some sort of a mistake. I would have to go and look at my list of transactions and see how much I actually should have. I pressed a few buttons and got up a mini statement and my shock turned to anger.

My balance was correct. The bank hadn't made a mistake. Rafael had paid me for the week I spent at his sister's wedding event. I hit the button to return my card and I stormed from the store, our dinner forgotten. I marched to Rafael's building and went up to his floor. I walked down the corridor to his office. I didn't bother to knock when I reached it. Fuck that. I didn't care who heard what I had to say.

Rafael looked up from his desk when I opened the office door. He started to smile and stopped when he saw my expression. Even then, when I was so angry I could throttle him, I couldn't help but appreciate how gorgeous he was. But I wasn't going to let that distract me.

"What the fuck Rafael?" I said. He looked confused, like he had no idea what I was talking about. "The fee for the wedding?"

"Oh shit. Has it still not cleared yet. I'm sorry I thought it would have gotten through escrow today," he said. "Let me call the bank."

"What?" I demanded. "No. It cleared. I can't believe you did that. You treated me like some sort of whore."

"What? No, I didn't. God, Lena, I didn't mean it to seem that way at all. I sent it because we had a deal and it seemed wrong to not send it, like I would be taking advantage of you. I mean if you had still worked here and we had sex, you still would have wanted your wages right?" Rafael said.

"Oh come on Rafael, that's completely different and you know it," I shouted.

"Is it?" he said. "Because from where I'm standing, it's exactly the same. You were being paid to do a job and ..."

He was still talking but I could no longer hear him. I bent double as the most intense pain I had ever felt in my life ripped through my insides. I felt as though someone's hand was in there squeezing my internal organs while wearing a glove studded with broken glass. I needed to scream, but the most I could manage was a whimper.

Oh my God. I was going to die and the last conversation I had had with Rafael would have been a stupid argument about something that didn't even matter in the big scheme of things.

Another pulse of pain went through me, and tears coursed down my face as I whimpered again.

"Lena? Lena? What's wrong?" I heard Rafael saying.

It sounded as though his voice was coming from miles away rather than from beside me. I tried to answer him, but I couldn't speak. I felt myself tumbling towards the ground and then I felt Rafael's strong arms around me. He caught me before I hit the floor and he held me in his arms. I tried to tell him I was sorry, but it was too late. Everything went black.

RAFAEL

J ran from my office with Lena in my arms. I debated calling nine one one, but I was convinced that I could get her to the nearest hospital quicker than waiting for an ambulance to come out and I had to get her there quickly, I knew that much. I had no idea what was wrong with her, but I couldn't lose her. I just couldn't.

I went down in the elevator, mumbling at it to hurry up the whole time it was going down, and the second the doors opened, I rushed across the foyer. One of the night security guards called after me asking if everything was ok but I didn't stop running; I didn't even slow down to answer him, I just shouted no and kept on running. I got to my car and unlocked it and laid Lena down on the back seat. I slammed the back door and wrenched the front door open, and I jumped into the driver's seat and pulled away with a squeal of tires.

I left the parking lot and I forced myself to drive sensibly. If I went too fast, Lena could get thrown to the floor, or I could get pulled over and waste precious time. Or I could lose control of the car and hit a lamp post and kill us both. I drove a few miles an hour over the speed limit. It wasn't exactly late but it also wasn't exactly early either and the roads were a lot quieter than they would have been a few hours ago which made it slightly easier for me to move quickly, but there was still enough traffic that it slowed me down. That was the part where waiting for an ambulance would have had an advantage. The sirens would have been going and other drivers would have moved out of the way for us. And of course, the paramedics could have already been treating Lena.

Finally, after what felt like a life time but was truthfully only five minutes or less, I saw the hospital up in front of me. I couldn't resist speeding up once it was in sight, and I practically took the corner into the hospital grounds on two wheels. I drove up to the ER entrance and threw my car into park. I got out and went to the back and scooped Lena out. I didn't even stop to close the doors of the car; I just ran into the ER.

"Can I get some help here please," I shouted as I ran in.

Several people in the waiting room looked up and then looked away again quickly, pleased that my emergency wasn't theirs. The triage nurse who manned the reception desk was on her feet having already hit the alarm. She ran over to me.

"What happened?" she asked.

"I don't really know," I said. "One minute she was fine and then the next minute, she was bent double, holding her stomach, in too much pain to talk and then she just collapsed."

By the time I explained a.it to the triage nurse, a doctor, two nurses and someone with a trolley had appeared beside me and heard what I had to say. I laid Lena on the trolley, and she was instantly wheeled away. I started to follow them but one of the nurses blocked my path.

"You'll have to wait out here sir," she said.

"But …" I started.

"Please sir," she said. "The more time I spend debating with you, the less time I spend with your wife."

I didn't bother to correct her, I just nodded my head and backed off. The nurse scurried away, and I went back out of the ER to move my car. I debated calling Lena's mom, but until I knew more, I decided not to. It would only panic her, and I had no real information to give her anyway.

I parked my car in the parking lot. I had been kind of surprised it was still there after I ran inside and left the doors open and the keys in the ignition. I suppose something had to go right this evening. I jogged back to the ER room and went to sit down in the waiting room.

I hadn't been sat down for long when the nurse who stopped me from following Lena appeared in the waiting room. She beckoned to me, and I followed her to a private room where she gestured for me to sit down.

"Is she ok?" I asked.

"She has been sent for emergency surgery on her abdomen. The doctor has advised that you go up to the surgical ward to wait because that's where she will be sent after the operation and the surgeon will be able to fill you in on what's happening," the nurse said. "You may stay in here for as long as you need to in the meantime."

With that she was gone. I took a minute and I sat with my face in my hands. God how had this gone so wrong? Lena was young and fit and healthy. What the hell had happened to her? I shook my head. I had no idea and speculating was doing nothing but scaring me more. All I knew was that Lena had to be ok. She had to be. Because the thought of losing her had made me realize that I never wanted to lose her. I had fallen completely, hopelessly in love with the woman that three short weeks ago, I would have said I hated with a passion.

LENA

I woke up slowly as though I was wading through treacle. The last time I had felt so deeply asleep was the morning after Rafael and I had sex for the first time, but this felt different. For starters, my stomach was hurting and there was a beeping sound coming from beside me. It must be my alarm clock. I reached out to turn it off, but nothing happened, and I finally opened my eyes.

I took in the sterile looking white ceiling and walls, and the blue blanket that covered me to my chest where a white and blue spotted gown took over, and it dawned on me that I was in hospital. But why?

I tried to sit up and a sharp pain went through my stomach, and I flopped back down with a groan.

"Hey, don't try to move yet," Rafael said.

I felt relief flood me. He was here. Even after I had yelled at him, he had stayed. I felt tears fill my eyes.

"Are you in pain?" Rafael asked, his face lined with concern.

"No," I said, my voice barely louder than a whisper. "Well, yes, but that's not why I'm crying."

"What is it?" he asked.

"You stayed," I said. "I was a bitch to you, I completely over reacted, and you stayed."

"Of course I stayed," Rafael said with a soft laugh. "It'll take a bit more than that to get rid of me."

"Good to know," I joked, and we both laughed but I instantly regretted it as my stomach tugged with pain. I winced. "What happened?"

"I'm not sure. The nurse said just to sit in here with you and the surgeon will be around soon," he said.

"I had surgery?" I said.

"Oh. Yes. Sorry I thought you knew that. I don't know why though," Rafael said.

I pressed the bell for a nurse. I needed to know what the hell was going on with me. A nurse came along a few minutes later and she smiled down at me.

"Ah, you're awake. Let me get Doctor Patterson to come in and speak to you," she said.

She left before I could ask her any questions and I hoped this Doctor Patterson wasn't going to pull the same stunt. I didn't have to wait long to find out. Doctor Patterson came into the room a few minutes later. He was younger looking than I would have expected a surgeon to be. He had blonde floppy hair and blue eyes and a rather large nose.

"Hello Ms Rogers," he said, smiling at me.

"Call me Lena," I croaked. "How do you know my name anyway?"

"I told them," Rafael said.

Oh of course. The anesthetic must have left me a bit dozy I thought to myself.

"How are you feeling?" Doctor Patterson asked.

I shrugged.

"I've been better but overall, not too bad," I said.

"That's good," he said. "Considering it was pretty much

touch and go back there. Your appendix had burst. Another two, three minutes and you would have gone into septic shock. We most likely would have lost you."

I took a minute to take that in, but Doctor Patterson wasn't finished dropping bombs on me just yet.

"Don't worry. There's no reason you won't make a fast and full recovery, and the baby is fine," he said.

"Umm baby?" I said.

"Ah. You didn't know. I wasn't sure you would with it being so early," he said. "When you get out of here, make an appointment with your usual doctor and you can start thinking about choosing an OB-GYN if you don't already have one."

"Wait, I think you have me mixed up with someone else. I'm not pregnant," I said. "I'm on birth control."

"I can assure you that you very much are pregnant Ms ... Lena. Birth control isn't one hundred percent effective as I'm sure you know. Now if you'll excuse me, I have to be in surgery in half an hour," Doctor Patterson said and then he too was gone leaving me with a ton of questions.

I took a deep breath and thought for a moment. Pregnant. I didn't know how I felt about it. I put my hands on my stomach and I felt myself starting to smile. Ok, I knew how I felt about it. I was happy. Me. The woman who had never wanted children was happy to be expecting one. But I knew I couldn't expect Rafael to sign up to this. We had been together less than a month after all. I turned my head towards him.

"You don't have to be a part of this Rafael," I said. "Honestly, I won't hold it against you. I know we haven't been together long and ..."

He reached out and gently brushed his fingers on my lips in a shush gesture. I stopped talking and looked at him.

"Admittedly you tried a bit harder to get rid of me this

time, but I've told you Lena, I'm not going anywhere. And please don't think I am only staying with you because you're pregnant. Don't get me wrong I am excited at the thought of being a father, but I am staying because well ... because I love you, Lena," he said.

Tears filled me eyes and I blinked them away and swallowed hard past the lump that had suddenly formed in my throat.

"I love you too," I whispered.

He leaned forward and kissed me on the lips and in that moment, despite the fact I was in hospital and had just had surgery, everything was right in the world.

EPILOGUE – Rafael
Ten Months Later

My grandmother looked up from the baby's face and smiled at me and Lena.

"She is adorable," she confirmed. "A real beauty. Are you sure about the name though?"

"I couldn't think of anyone I would rather my daughter be named after," Lena said. "And Evelyn is such a pretty name."

My grandmother beamed at her and then looked back down at the baby.

"And to think, when I first met your mom, she and your dad were playing some silly game where they pretended to be dating even though they didn't like each other. I suspect that might have been to make an old lady happy. And here we are. They finally saw it wasn't an act after all and now the old lady is very happy indeed."

"What?" I exclaimed. "You knew all along?"

"Of course I did Raf. I'm old not stupid. No one else picked up on it, but that's because they don't see what's right in front of them," she said.

"Why didn't you say anything?" I asked.

"Because I could see that something was starting to form between you two and if I had told you the game was up, you would have had no reason to continue to spend time together. And this little poppet would never have been born," my grandmother said.

I shook my head in wonder, although in hindsight, I should never have underestimated her like that. If anyone was going to know what was really going on in any given situation, it was her.

Lena and I had lunch with my grandmother while baby Evelyn slept, and afterwards, we took a stroll along the street in front of my grandmother's house.

"You do remember our deal, don't you?" I said. "If my grandmother suspects anything, the deal is off? So, I do believe you owe me a substantial amount of money."

"Yeah, you're too late buddy. See someone persuaded me to use it to buy my own day care centre," Lena said, nudging me and smiling.

"That was good advice," I said laughing. "But about your debt. If you can't pay it in money, well there are other ways."

I raised an eyebrow and Lena playfully slapped me on the arm. We laughed and I wrapped an arm around her, and she snuggled against me and it was the three of us against the world, and in that moment, my whole world was absolutely perfect.

THE END

Enjoyed this story?

Head on over to **Amazon** to leave a review.

DID YOU LIKE THIS STORY?

Here's a sneak peak of my next book

***

MY ENEMY BILLIONAIRE PROTECTOR

A Pretend Relationship Forced Proximity Age Gap Romance

***

MY ENEMY BILLIONAIRE PROTECTOR

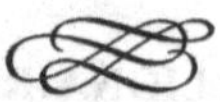

OWEN

I let out a deep sigh as I stir under my sheet. It's warming up now as we move into spring, and I don't need a heavy duvet to snuggle under anymore. I always wake up a minute before my alarm goes off, and sure enough, it starts screaming.

I turn it off, get up, and rub the sleep from my eyes before I go to relieve myself and take a shower. The hot water wakes me up as I use my body wash to wash everything, including my hair.

I step out of the shower and towel dry myself before I brush my teeth and get ready for work. I eye the stubble on my face, but I guess I could shave tonight or tomorrow morning. I hear the coffee machine automatically turn on and sigh again. Every day, I do the same thing. I love routine but even I'm getting a little bored.

I'm looking forward to the conference that's coming up. Since I launched my franchise opportunity for the Bendy Pets franchise, it's been steadily growing, and I'm making a lot of profit from it. Who knew that animal chiropractic specialists would be so in demand?

I flick a switch, and the curtains slide open automatically. It's good to be in a big home again. I wouldn't say I spoiled myself, but I did give myself a place I'm proud of. I'm not going to make my father's mistakes though. I won't lose what I've worked so hard to build. That's why I need to stay focused and dedicated to the business.

Once I'm dressed and I've downed an espresso, I leave. I climb into my Mercedes and drive toward the practice I opened, the first of a long list spreading across the states. My mind is occupied by numbers and meetings when I check the date.

Dammit.

It's Bella's day.

I *cannot* stand Bella, the young woman my head therapist hired for the practice. I suppose she's competent at her job, but she's constantly rude and defiant. She thinks she is the boss rather than the other way around.

As I pull into my parking spot, I see her through the front windows of the practice. I grab my briefcase and go inside.

"Good morning, everyone," I greet.

Two customers, a therapist, and Bella are in the waiting room. Everyone greets me but her greeting instantly irritates me.

I set my things down in my office and come out to see that everything is running correctly and processes are being followed. I see Bella is making out a receipt, and I step closer.

She glances at me with a raised eyebrow.

I wait until the customer has left before I lean over and take the receipt book. "You're still not making the receipts out properly."

"Good morning, Mr. Seawright," she says. "This is how I was told to do them. Therefore, this is how I am doing them."

"Well, they're wrong," I say grumpily. "You're using the

wrong numbers for the reference number. You get the reference number from here."

I log onto the computer and show her, and she nods.

"This client doesn't have an account yet. According to Charlie, the other receptionist, if I haven't set up an account, I can use their account number."

I am about to say something else but then close my mouth. "You should set up accounts immediately when the client arrives."

Before she can argue, I go back to my office and busy myself with the accounts of the franchise. I have a twelve o'clock lunch that I cannot miss and want to be done by then.

As the minutes tick by, I hear Bella greeting clients in that Southern twang of hers when they walk in. I don't mind Southerners, but I mind her. I just don't feel like she's a good fit.

I shut my door as I work, and I'm slightly startled when there's a knock. Dr. Charlie Slip sticks his head in. "Ready for lunch?"

"Is it that time already?" I smile and get up. I then go over and shake his hand. "Haven't seen you all week."

"I know, it's been busy. I'm excited about the sushi though. I hear they're having an all-you-can-eat special." He grins, and I grab my car keys.

I lead him out into reception, and he leans over the counter to speak to Bella. "We're going out for lunch. We'll be back in an hour or so."

"Noted, Dr. Slip," she says with a smile. She then gives me a cold look before looking back at her computer screen.

We climb into my car, and Charlie chuckles. "She still doesn't like you?"

"She's not a good fit for the practice," I huff.

"Owen, you're the most dominant macho man I know.

Don't be scared of a little Texan girl." Charlie is teasing, but I roll my eyes anyway.

"I'm not scared. I just don't think she fits in."

"She fits in well not only because she does her job well, despite what you believe, but because she's really smart and interested in what we do."

"Sure," I say, waving him off.

I drive us to our favorite restaurant and find parking. There is no wait so we are quickly seated.

Charlie, of course, asks for several dishes of sushi while I order a steak with steamed vegetables and a baked potato.

"At least this year we're not scraping by to attend the conference," Charlie says in between bites of sushi. "And it's on an island, beachfront and everything. It's going to be so relaxing."

"We're there to find potential clients," I say, cutting into my steak. "Don't lose sight of the goal."

"Yes. You and your goals. Can you not admit we're doing well? That your idea is brilliant and it's flourishing?" He shovels more sushi into his mouth, and I wrinkle my nose.

"I don't know how you can eat that stuff," I say.

"Because it's delicious. Want to try some?" he offers.

"No, thanks." I shake my head. "I prefer my meat red."

Charlie laughs. "Suit yourself."

I take a sip of my water, and he clears his throat.

"You wanted to talk about the conference?" Charlie asks.

I nod. "Yes, we need to stick together. With your medical expertise and my business expertise, I feel like we can attract a lot more people into buying franchises. Not only will this secure jobs for so many people, but, as discussed, you'll have shares in each practice that opens." I smile. "It's genius."

"So you want us to present a united front?" Charlie pushes his plate away.

"Yes, no matter what." I finish my meal and push my plate away as well. "We can really go far with this, Charlie."

"Why were you arguing with Bella again this morning?" he asks, taking a sip of his wine.

I shake my head. "She wasn't doing her job properly. I mean, I should expect that."

"Why? She does amazing. She could run that practice blindfolded!" Charlie chuckles. "What have you got against a beautiful and sassy woman?"

"I don't have an issue with sassy, beautiful women. She doesn't do a good job. She constantly flouts processes and disrespects me as much as she physically can without getting fired. She's exactly my brother's type." I shake my head and look away, signaling the waitress to refill our drinks.

"Oh, so it's because she's your brother's ex-girlfriend? That's rather unfair to judge her on that." Charlie nods at the waitress, signaling his thanks.

I snort. "Anyone who is dumb enough to be attracted to my brother is not someone I want to employ for my company."

"Only *I* employed her, you didn't. And I still have a say." He raises an eyebrow at me, and I let out an irritated sigh.

"Why? What is so special about her that a thousand girls can't replace her?"

"Because even if I hired a thousand girls, they couldn't keep up with her. Give her a chance, Owen. You might even come to find you like her a little." Charlie chuckles. He puts a fist to his chest slightly. "Hmmm, heartburn. I'll be back."

He goes to the bathroom, and I sigh. I think about Bella and how I'm not overly fond of her. You can tell a lot about a person by the company they keep, and my brother, Lance, is a real piece of work. He's taken so much from me, like two of my business ideas to get ahead, and he will always do that. It's why I've distanced myself from him. He's toxic. If Bella can date someone that toxic, then I can only reasonably assume she is toxic too, and I don't want that in my practice.

Charlie comes back, looking a bit flushed. "The heartburn is horrible. Do you mind if we go?"

"Not at all. I'll pay the check on the way out." I stand and finish my drink before following Charlie to the front. I settle the bill, and we go straight to my car.

"You're not looking too great, Charlie. Did you eat too much?" I ask. "Cause if you're going to be sick, I'd rather call you an Uber."

He chuckles lightly. "No, I'm fine."

We drive back in silence, with Charlie groaning now and then. He's as close to a friend as I've got, so I worry about him. When we get back, I get out of the car and point in the direction of his car. "Go. Go to a doctor or go home and lie down. You're looking worse."

Charlie nods, his face looking bloated. "I think I'll go to the emergency doctor. Thanks, Owen, I'll let you know what happens."

He walks off, pausing now and then to issue a loud and disgusting burp. I shake my head and walk inside. As I pass Bella, I comment, "Charlie is off the rest of the day. He's not feeling well."

She smirks. "Too much beer for lunch?"

I whip around quickly. "Excuse me?"

She looks up at me. "I said, did he have too much beer? Beer makes him bloat, and he doesn't feel well after."

"It's none of your goddamn business, Bella. Your job is to work the front desk, not to monitor the lives of the doctors here. My office. *Now.*"

I storm to my office and slam the door open. She sashays in and puts her hands on her hips. "You don't have to speak to me like that when there are clients in the waiting room."

"You do not question your senior management," I snap.

"You are so rude and disrespectful. Who the hell do you think you are?"

"I know damn well who I am and how I should be spoken to, sir. There is no reason for you to raise your voice or get cocky with me. I give it as I get it. Since I was hired months ago, all you have given me is grief."

"Well, maybe it's because you're too incompetent to do your damn job. You spend so much time talking to people, chatting up a storm…"

"It's called *customer service*," she snaps. She then flings her hand up and points to the front. "I am the first person they see when they come in. They must be assured that this is a friendly environment they are bringing their pets into."

I shake my head. "I should damn well fire you."

"I'd like to see you try." She crosses her arms. "I'll call all three practicing doctors right now if that's what you want because I've already told them how you continue to harass me."

"I don't harass you," I snort. "I want you to do your job. God, you're so entitled."

"I do my job, and I do it well. I don't know why you hate me, but you best sort that out with yourself. You freaking Seawrights are all the same! You are all a bunch of jerks." She crosses her arms again. "Now, if you don't mind, I actually have work to do."

She storms out, and I flop into my chair. It's childish to argue like this. I know it. I should just fire her, but if she's already reporting to the others that I'm "harassing" her, then I need to build some evidence against her.

She really makes my blood boil. I can hear her now, talking to a client with that sweet voice that is just *too* sugary. She lays it on so thick.

There's a knock at my door, and I sit up straight. "Yes?"

One of the assistants walks in. "Hi, Mr. Seawright. We

need to place a huge order for supplies. We had a lot of unexpected emergencies, and we need to restock."

"David, right?" I smile. "You have a list?"

He walks forward and hands me the lengthy report.

"Okay, this shouldn't be a problem. You can have Katie order it for you."

"She's not here. Can I ask Bella?"

I frown. "Actually, I will place the order."

He looks at me hesitantly and then nods. "Okay, sir."

I log into our system and go to the necessary page for ordering supplies. I stare at his report. It's all shorthand and not something I'm familiar with.

I sigh and compose myself before I get up and go to the front desk. "Order this stuff for the back. They're running low."

I place the report on the desk, and Bella glances at me with a smile. "Yes, Mr. Seawright."

I hurry back to my office and shut the door. I'm just about to mumble to myself about her being a little prissy when my phone rings. I look at the caller ID, and my mood darkens.

"What now?" I ask as I answer the call.

"Is that how you answer all your calls? Your business won't fare well if you do that." My brother, Lance, sneers down the line. "Hello, Owen. How are you?"

"Lance, you're not calling to find out how I am. You want something. Just spit it out so I can get back to work." I sit at my desk and use my free hand to rub my temple.

"That's so rude," Lance exclaims. "I am genuinely interested in how you're doing. I haven't seen you in forever."

"That's because you don't bother to. I've invited you around a few times for a beer," I sigh. "Come on, what do you want this time?"

"It's not what I want so much as what I need. I wanted to know if you could loan me half a million to get a new start-up off the ground. Of course, I'll pay you back with interest. You can even have the contract drawn up yourself." I can hear something in the background, and it takes me a while to recognize the noise.

"Are you calling me while you're playing golf?" I ask.

"I'm putting in a quick few holes with the men I hope will invest with me." He chuckles and then shouts, "Good shot!"

I frown and shake my head. "I'm not giving you the money, Lance. You still owe me almost three million from all the loans I've taken out and money I've given you that you *promised* to pay back."

"We need to put the past behind us, Owen. I am happy to sign a contract to ensure you get your money back."

"No," I say firmly. "It's not happening, so I suggest you find some other idiot to fund your lifestyle because it won't be me."

"You're my brother, Owen," he says quietly. "We're supposed to look out for each other."

"Yeah, and how have you looked out for me, Lance?" I growl. "Aside from using me as much as you physically can over the years. No, I won't give you a cent."

"Well, at least let's catch up…"

"I don't have time. I'm at work," I snip.

"Do you have a girlfriend yet? Maybe someone to spend your days with?" he asks.

I frown. It's not like Lance to ask about my personal life.

"What does it matter to you? Even if I have someone, it's not like I would introduce her to you. You'd probably try to take her too. You'll try to take every last thing I own, but it's not going to happen, Lance. The gravy train has been decommissioned and is no longer running on the railway."

Lance chuckles. "I always did love your little analogies, Owen. Just consider my proposal. I'll even give you proper shares in the start-up. It'll be a passive income for you while I do all the work. There's nothing to it."

"You haven't done a day's work in your life unless wheeling and dealing is now considered a career. I will never understand how you can afford your lifestyle, but enjoy it and leave me out of it."

I hang up the phone and toss it onto the table with a sigh. I can feel the tension between my shoulder blades just from speaking to my brother. It's ridiculous the amount of influence he has over my stress levels. However, I'm sticking to what I've said. I'm not funding his little lifestyle anymore. All our siblings do. We all give in to him, and it needs to come to a stop.

MY ENEMY BILLIONAIRE PROTECTOR

BELLA

*L*ord have mercy, I hate that man so damn much. I am so glad he wasn't the one who interviewed me for this job; otherwise, I would not have been hired. He seems to have had a gripe with me since the day I started, and he realized I used to date Lance.

His brother is a jerk and so is he. I cannot stand their entire family, and I don't even know all of them.

However, I don't want to push Owen too far because I know he is the person I'm going to have to get through when I want to buy my own franchise of Bendy Pets.

I don't think he realizes that's what I want to do or that I often get called in by therapists to learn and help. Of course, I told them all that I wanted to study further and become a pet chiropractor. I have always been passionate about animals and would love to do something like this.

Unlike Owen, though, I don't come from a life of luxury and money, so I have to do things the old-fashioned way and work hard. I doubt he knows anything about working hard. All he does is try to control me, and he's so overbearing and cocky.

I can tell he was a bad boy back in the day, much like Lance, but he does have something Lance lacks and that's leadership. Where Lance would be an omega, Owen is definitely an alpha. He takes charge and makes decisions. It must be so nice to make decisions without worrying if it will cost you your next meal.

"Bella?"

I turn to see Dr. Holly Drake standing at her door. "Want to come see me help a dog walk better?"

I look around. There's no one else in the waiting room. "Sure."

I put a "be right back" sign on my desk and hurry to the patient room. There's a senior Swiss shepherd there, and my heart melts instantly. "Oh, hey, there, darling Winter. Are you ready for your adjustment?"

Holly smiles and positions herself. "Now remember, you want to do a *quick* correction, but don't be afraid or hesitate because you could hurt them. Winter here has had some trouble walking, and a slight adjustment to her spine should alleviate that a little."

Dr. Holly holds the dog along the spine. There's a loud crackle as the doctor makes a quick movement. Winter yelps because she's startled, but she's not in pain. Winter looks around, confused. She takes a hesitant step forward and then another, and her tail starts wagging like crazy. For some odd reason, she comes straight to me, and I gladly pet her.

I walk the client out and stand at the front desk. "It's amazing. She's walking like a brand new dog."

Holly smiles as she fills in Winter's paperwork. "If they come every two weeks or so, Winter's quality of life can be improved for a year or more. They'll have more precious time with her."

"Ain't that something," I sigh. "I can't wait until I know how to do these things and have my own practice."

"You're not going to get it if you don't mention it to Owen," she teases.

Everyone knows how Owen and I butt heads, but I am optimistic he will take me more seriously and respect me once I am a therapist.

I smile as the door opens but then my smile falters as Owen walks in. He frowns at me before he smiles at Holly. "Dr. Drake, it's always lovely to see you."

"Mr. Seawright," she greets him with a nod.

He doesn't say anything to me, and I look at the time.

"You know, if you were a little more polite, it might help." Holly is trying to say it as gently as possible, but I still roll my eyes.

"That man has no manners for me. What I get is what I give. Now, I'm clocking out. I have plans tonight, and I have plans before my plans."

"Still waiting for your acceptance letter?" Holly asks as I pack up my things.

"Believe me, there will be signs I got it." I grin. "Now, if I don't hurry, I'll miss the bus. I'll see you later." I grab my bag and hurry out.

She calls her goodbyes.

I'm thankful I don't have to lock up, but I flip the sign on the door before I shut the door behind me.

Closed.

One day, I'll flip the sign on my own franchise, and it'll say "Open for Business."

Maybe I'll even have a little ribbon ceremony and everything.

I walk down the road, lost in my thoughts, when a drizzle starts coming down. I hurry to get under the bus shelter and wait there for the bus that is never on time.

I look around, keeping a keen eye on my surroundings. I

don't trust anyone, even if we're in a nice part of the city. Where I'm from, a woman must know how to care for herself.

The bus pulls up, and the doors open. I find my seat and put my left earbud in to listen to my favorite animal podcast while still being aware of my surroundings.

The bus trundles along through the drizzle, and I relax a little once the last passenger is off the bus. I'm almost at my apartment, and a nervous excitement is building within me. I cannot wait to see if I finally have my letter. I just need to know. Good or bad. I need the answer.

I thank the driver as I hop off. I hurry through the rain, up the road, and into my apartment building. I pause at the mailboxes and open mine. There are many things in there, so I grab them all and hurry upstairs to the second floor. Once I unlock it, I quickly shut the door behind me. I toss my bag down and start scrambling through the envelopes, but there's nothing with the university logo.

My shoulders sink, and I sigh. I toss the rest of the mail into the bowl near the door to be looked at tomorrow.

I strip off my clothes and toss them in the hamper before I get the shower running nice and hot. I let the hot water soak into my skin for a few minutes before I wash and rinse my hair and then wash my body. We're going out tonight for drinks, and we probably will go partying. I can't stay out too late or get too drunk because I have work tomorrow. I also have to prepare because Dr. Slip and Owen will attend an exotic island conference while the lowly servants remain back and work hard.

God, it's so frustrating.

I dry off, dry my hair, curl it, and slip into tight jeans and a crop top. I only put on a little makeup to sharpen and highlight my features. Drying my bum-length black hair and curling it took too long, and now I'm running late. I hurry out the door. Thankfully, it isn't raining anymore. I hail a taxi and hop in, asking for it to take me to Mickey's Dive, a local bar we like to visit near the club.

The cab driver plays old classics on the radio, like Frank Sinatra, and I almost want to giggle. I suppose that's the kind of music Owen would listen to. I can't wait to tell the girls all about him tonight.

I pay the driver after I get out, and I walk toward the pub. A few people are mingling outside, talking loudly. I bypass them to get inside to the back where my friends have a table already.

"Bella!" the girls shriek, throwing their hands in the air. They've obviously already started drinking. I sit down, and my friend Dawn flags down a waitress, "A Vodka cranberry please."

The waitress smiles and hurries off, and Dawn turns to me. "I've needed this night so bad. Work has been a nightmare."

"It's all she can say," Robin says with a giggle. "It must be *so* hard being the CEO of your beauty brand business."

"When it takes off properly, and you're rolling in the billions, then come talk to me," I raise my voice to be heard over the loud music and talking around us.

Layla scoots to the right so I can sit next to her. These are the first three friends I made when I moved up from Texas, and we've been best friends since then.

"How is bone cracking going?" Dawn asks, passing me my drink from the waitress before she pays for it.

I nod. "It's going well except for Seawright, of course. Owen is such a douche."

"That's because he's rolling in money." Dawn smiles. "I promise not to become a douche when I'm rich."

"Same," we all chorus.

We then clink our glasses together before laughing. I sip my drink and sigh.

"He keeps saying I don't do my job properly when everyone knows I do. I swear he's picking on me because I broke up with Lance." I look around. "Obviously, he feels he needs to avenge his brother."

"Fuck them all," Layla calls suddenly and then giggles.

"How much have you had to drink?" Robin asks.

"A couple. I had a work lunch function and then came straight here." She gives us a goofy grin, and I snort.

"She's going to have to dance it off on the dance floor cause she's already cooked." I sip my drink and glance around.

Something, or rather, *someone*, catches my eye, and I groan quietly.

The girls hear me, and all look in the same direction. Lance is at the bar with a blonde, rather big-breasted, smiley woman.

"I've suddenly lost the will to dance," I grumble.

"You can't hide from him forever," Robin comments. "And especially now because he's seen you and is coming over."

I straighten my features and smile before I turn to look up at Lance.

"Bella. You're looking good." He smiles.

I stand because I don't want him leaning over me.

"What do you want, Lance?" I ask, sipping my drink. "We're about to head out."

"Aw, come on. You're not still angry with me, are you?" He holds out his hands, and I can literally feel the slime dripping off his words.

I set my drink down and step out of my seat. "Actually, I was just headed home. Can't have fun knowing the kind of people out and about."

On cue, my friends rise, and the waitress comes over.

Dawn pays the bill, and we move past Lance and the smiling girl who seems confused. We walk outside, and when the fresh air hits us, Layla doubles over.

"Perhaps tonight is not the night for dancing," Dawn concedes.

"Do you want a lift, Bella?" Robin asks. "I'm taking Dawn and Layla home."

"It's okay." I smile. "I'll grab a cab. I'm in the opposite direction. Thanks, though. I'll text you when I'm home."

So much for a fun night out...

When I walk toward the office in the morning, I'm still seething about Lance trying to be so friendly. Owen had better not start with me today because I don't know if I can remain composed.

I open the door, and Dr. Drake stands at reception, looking excited. "The one day I have something exciting to tell you, and you're not here early."

"Bus was late," I comment, confused. "What's happened?"

"Dr. Slip had to call out of the conference because he has food poisoning!" she squeals.

I chuckle. "So you get to go?"

"No!" she shrieks. "*You* do!"

I am floored. "What?"

"You're the only one we can spare with enough medical know-how to speak to people. Owen wasn't happy about it at first, but Dr. Slip made sure he understood he had no choice. You're going to the conference, Bella. You can show Owen how much you know and make connections while you're there." Holly grabs my arms and jumps up and down, but when she sees I'm not doing the same, she pauses. "I thought you'd be excited."

I give a half smile. "I... I mean, I am. It's just so sudden." The nerves hit me, and I bite my lip. "What if I mess this up? What if I'm no good? Owen will fire me."

Holly frowns and takes my hands in hers, giving them a squeeze. "You're going to do amazing because you were born to do this, right?"

I take a deep breath and nod. "Right."

"You're going to become a therapist one day. These are the kinds of things they will call on you to do. Dr. Mills and I are fully booked, so we can't take off to go with Owen. You're going to represent us, you're going to do a fantastic job, *and* you get to visit an exotic island." She beams at me.

"Wait, isn't the conference tomorrow?" I ask with wide eyes.

"That's right, so you need to go home and pack. Your flight is in two and a half hours. I'll call you a cab, so don't worry about the cost," Holly says before hurrying off.

I look to reception where the other two receptionists are beaming at me. I feel a bit dazed, to be honest. I didn't expect this. Holly comes back to tell me the cab is on its way. She gives me a hug. "I have to go to work but text me photos every day. I want to know everything that happens."

I smile. "Okay. I'll see you soon."

Holly hurries off, and I go back outside to wait for my cab. Everything seems to pass in a blur, and soon enough, I'm in my apartment packing. I don't know what to wear.

I'm not rich. I don't own fancy clothes. I pick out my most respectable-looking work clothes and carefully pack them. I also pack in some beachwear in case we get some downtime to see the ocean. That would be lovely…

Fuck! I'm going to an exotic island. I can't believe it. I don't even care that I have to go with Owen and work alongside him. I get a text message from work saying that the cab is on its way to collect me to take me to the airport. Everything has been arranged. I just have to bring my passport.

I squeal and hurry to finish packing. I change into a smart casual outfit and make sure everything is locked up so I can hurry downstairs. I wait on the curb, excitedly looking up and down the road when a yellow cab pulls up in front of me.

"Miss Underwood-Knox?" the driver asks, getting out to help me with my bags.

"Yes, thank you." I climb into the back and settle in. I fidget with my hair. I only packed a romance book to read on the plane. I might need to buy another at the airport so I don't get bored while I ignore Owen.

I've never seen him work with investors. I wonder if he's as slimy as Lance is. Probably. They are brothers, after all.

As we pull up to the airport, the cab driver refuses payment. "It is on the company account."

I insist on giving him a tip though, and he thanks me as he loads my bag onto a cart. I push it through the airport and consult the message on my phone. The gate is on the other side of the airport, so I stop where I know there is a bookstore to get three books, a crossword puzzle book, and a pencil.

I continue my walk down the corridors, but there are fewer and fewer people as I go. I'm starting to feel a bit wary as I move into what looks like a more privately owned section.

"Ma'am, you're not allowed to be here," a hostess says, walking over to me. "This section of the airport is for private travelers."

"I was told to come to Gate 19C," I say, looking around. "If you can point me in that direction, I'll gladly head back so I don't miss my flight."

She looks confused and looks at my phone. "Ah, you're on Mr. Morgan's plane. You are taking a private flight. I apologize for my mistake. You just go down two more gates, and it's to your left. There is a hostess there who can assist you. Enjoy your flight."

Did I hear her right? A *private* flight? I try not to squeal again, especially now that I'm in public. However, I'm beaming as I hurry along.

"Miss Underwood-Knox?" asks the hostess at the gate.

"That's me."

"You can leave your luggage here to be checked by the luggage porter. You are sitting in business class with Mr. Seawright. He said you are to board immediately so he can prepare you."

"Prepare me for what?" I ask curiously, but the young lady simply shrugs and shakes her head.

I follow her to the plane. I've never walked on the runway before, and there aren't many planes around, but these seem big.

We're walking to a huge-looking one, and I follow the hostess up the stairs. She points me to my seat, and I walk there quietly, opening the above-head compartment to stow my carry-on.

"Why are you so late?"

Owen's voice makes me jump, and I look at him before shutting the compartment.

"I only got told that I was chosen to go when I got to work this morning. I had to pack and stuff."

I sit in my seat. It's luxurious, and I know I'll never fly in a fancy way again, so I intend to enjoy *every* second of it.

He glowers but turns away without a comment.

I watch him put his earphones on and turn a movie on. I tap him, and he glares at me. "What?"

"I thought you wanted to tell me what I had to do?" I ask.

"We can discuss it when we land or maybe over lunch. Right now, this is the only time I get to relax, and I want to enjoy it." He sits back and sighs.

I turn away and settle in my seat. I sigh as I look out the window.

What an adventure…

. . .

To continue reading, click HERE.

ABOUT THE AUTHOR

Everleigh Green has a passion for steamy contemporary romance stories focusing on forced proximity, fake fiancés, secret babies, and Billionaires with a capital 'B'. When not furiously typing away on her keyboard in NYC, she enjoys spending time with the cutest dog in the world, Cara, discovering new cooking recipes and watching old episodes of 'Law & Order'... All spin-offs.